TEEN TITANS GO!™

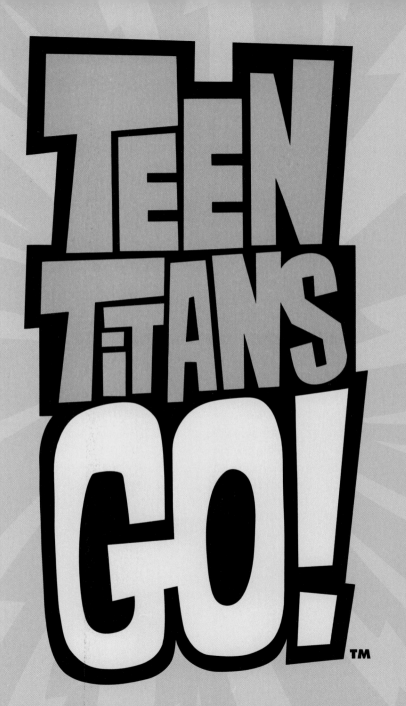

Little, Brown and Company
Hachette Book Group
1290 Avenue of the Americas, New York, NY 10104
Visit us at LBYR.com

First Edition: November 2017

Little, Brown and Company is a division of Hachette Book Group, Inc. The Little, Brown name and logo are trademarks of Hachette Book Group, Inc.

The publisher is not responsible for websites (or their content) that are not owned by the publisher.

Library of Congress Control Number 2017946358

ISBNs: 978-0-316-55776-4 (pbk.), 978-0-316-55780-1 (ebook), 978-0-316-55779-5 (ebook), 978-0-316-55778-8 (ebook)

Printed in the United States of America

CW

10 9 8 7 6 5 4 3 2 1

ROAD TRIPPIN'

Adapted by **Jonathan Evans**

Based on the episode "Road Trip"

written by **Marly Halpern-Graser**

LITTLE, BROWN AND COMPANY
New York   Boston

Robin, Raven, Starfire, and Beast Boy are spending a dull day in Titans Tower when they notice an intoxicating aroma filling the room.

"Where's that smell coming from?" asks Robin, looking around for the source.

"Oh man, it's making my nose hungry! Let's find out," says Beast Boy.

The four teammates follow the smell to the garage, where Cyborg is standing next to something hidden under a sheet. "What are you doing?" Cyborg asks.

"We've come in search of the smell of the gods!" says Starfire.

"You must be talking about the new-new car smell," Cyborg replies as he unveils the new-and-improved T-Car. "Ta-dah!"

"I've been tweaking, tinkering, and straight-up *improverating* everything," he says, stroking the car like a pet.

"The engine purrs like a kitten....
"The suspension is springy like fresh bread....

"The steering handles like...a car. There's not much you can do with steering."

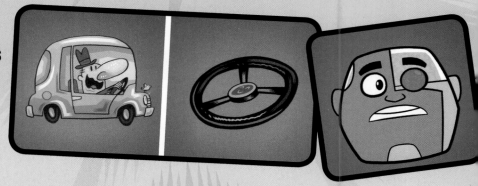

Starfire is concerned. "You act as if you have more affection for the car than for us," she says.

"Aw, I love you guys. But you have to understand: I took him in as a baby. I taught him karate, Spanish, and how to be a man," Cyborg explains.

Starfire is delighted that the car knows Spanish. "*Hola, Coche*," she says.
Robin bursts her bubble. "None of that was true, Star."

Cyborg ignores Robin. "I wish you guys could love this car the way I love him. *OOH!* I know what we're going to do...."

ROAD TRIP!

"Meh," says everyone else. Road trips seem boring.

"Aw, come on! Road trips are the most fun thing in the world. We'll bring snacks and bond as teammates. We'll drive from Point A to Point B, but it's not the destination that matters—*it's the journey!*"

"Snacks?" says Beast Boy.
"Team bonding?" says Robin.
"A magical journey?" says Starfire.
"*Woo!* Road trip!" they exclaim.

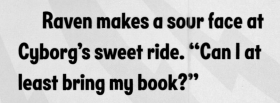

Raven makes a sour face at Cyborg's sweet ride. "Can I at least bring my book?"

THREE HOURS LATER...

"Are you guys having fun?" Cyborg asks.

"No," says Beast Boy. "We're out of snacks."

"There's been zero team bonding," adds Robin.

"I have not seen one fairy or the wizard on this magical journey," complains Starfire.

"And I'm starting to get carsick," says Raven.

Cyborg hates the whining. "Then stop reading in the car!" he yells.

Cyborg tries to be helpful. "Look, all road trips can get dull. That's what road games are for!"

Beast Boy has an idea. "Let's play Slug Bug!" He looks out the window, then punches Robin.

"*Gah!* All right, you got me," Robin laughs.

Starfire is alarmed. "Beast Boy, why would you do such a thing?"

"It's part of the game, Star," Robin explains. "Any time you see a bug go by, you yell 'SLUG BUG!' and hit someone."

"I understand." Starfire is pleased by the news and eager to join the fun.

A moment later, a bug flies past Robin's head. "SLUG BUG!" shouts Starfire as she punches Robin.

Then another bug splatters on the windshield. "SLUG BUG!" she cries, and punches him again.

"Ow! No, wrong kind of bug," cries Robin just as a swarm of insects appear out of nowhere. This is bad news for Robin.

"SLUG BUG!" "SLUG BUG!" "SLUG BUG!" "SLUG BUG!"

"What a delightful game!"
Starfire is jubilant as Robin
cries and asks her to cut it out.

Even Raven is amused.

Just then, Cyborg notices the villainous H.I.V.E. Five having car trouble up ahead.

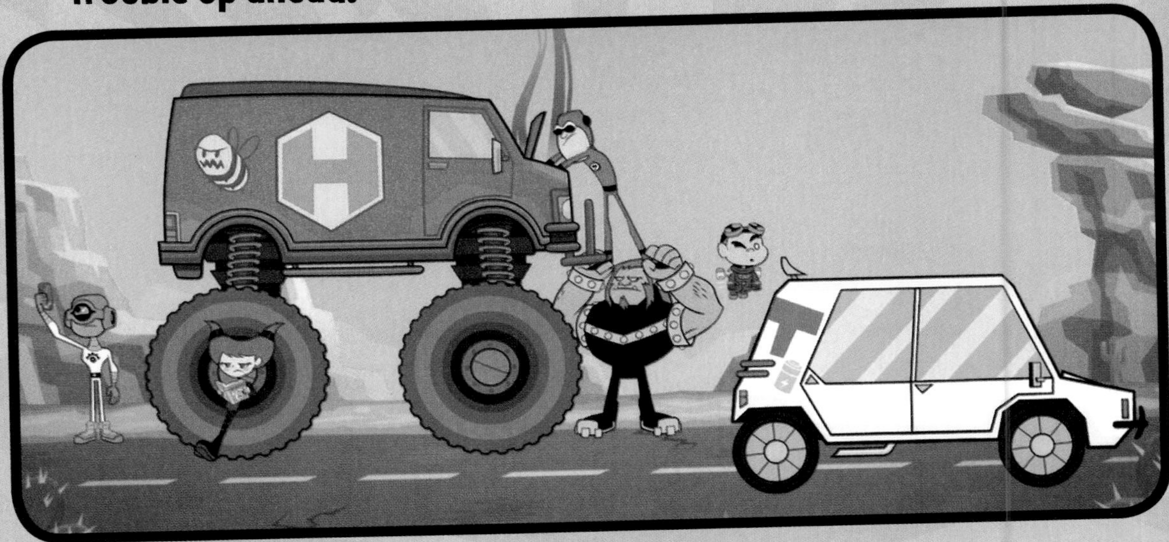

The Titans won't let them cause trouble—because they're going to cause it first! "Let's help them out. Hee-hee-hee..." Cyborg says.

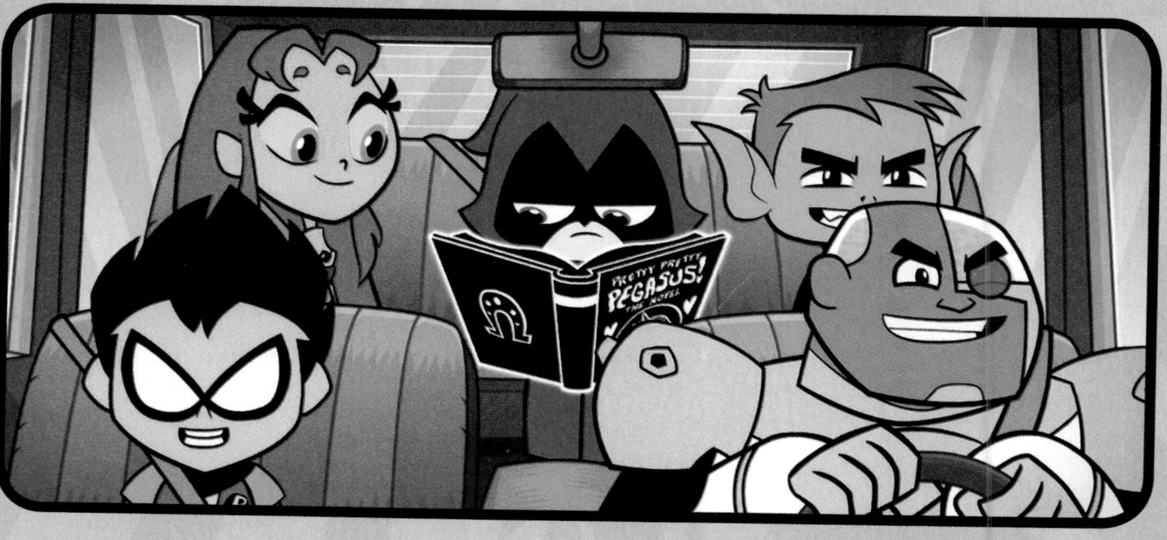
PRETTY PRETTY
PEGASUS!
THE NOVEL

"Hey, Gizmo, you need a ride to the mechanic?" Robin asks.

"Uh, sure. That's awful nice of you guys," Gizmo replies.

But before he can open the door, Cyborg hits the gas and leaves H.I.V.E. in the dust.

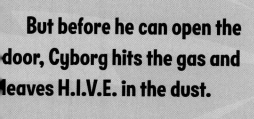

The team laughs as Beast Boy shouts, "I love road trips again!"

FIVE MINUTES LATER...

"Ugh, I'm bored again," complains Beast Boy.

Robin turns on the radio to break the silence.

"Uh-oh, look out... that's my jam!" he says as he starts dancing.

Cyborg quickly turns off the radio. "Uh-uh. We're not doing that."

Robin is annoyed. "Hey, I was getting my groove on. You see my cape flying?"

"No one wants to see your groove on. Take your groove off!" Cyborg yells as the car swerves into the opposite lane.

"SLUG BUG!" Starfire spots another bug and punches Beast Boy in the face.

"Why are there so many bugs in this car?" he cries.

Meanwhile, Raven's reading has finally caught up to her, and she's got a bad case of car sickness. Suddenly, she can't hold it anymore.

Cyborg is fed up. "That's it! Do you want to walk home?"
Turns out, they do. "You're really gonna walk?" Cyborg asks sadly.
"That was just an empty threat."

"Sorry, but we're done with the road trip," Raven says. The rest of the team angrily agrees with Raven.

"Who needs those guys?" Cyborg says to nobody in particular as he drive on. But eventually...Cyborg misses his friends, and he turns around.

The rest of the Titans, meanwhile, are melting under the midday desert sun when Cyborg pulls up.

"Hey, guys. Climb in. I'll drive you home."

"No, thanks," Beastie says.
"We're doing great,"
Robin adds.

"I'm sorry, guys. I just wanted you to love this car as much as I do," Cyborg says. "Plus, I've got air-conditioned seats."
Apology accepted.

Up the road, Cyborg notices something. It's H.I.V.E.! And they look angry.

"Get us out of here!" orders Robin as the H.I.V.E. car comes toward them with all its weapons blazing.

"We're gonna have to work together to get out of this one," says Cyborg. Robin is stoked. "That sounds like team bonding!"

"You wanna see some magic?" Cyborg asks Starfire as he presses a button to fire the T-Car's rocket engine. "Abracadabra!"

But H.I.V.E.'s monster truck has its own monster rocket engine.

It also has monster wheels and a monster cannon.

"I'm gonna need an assist here, Beastie," Cyborg says as he opens a secret compartment.

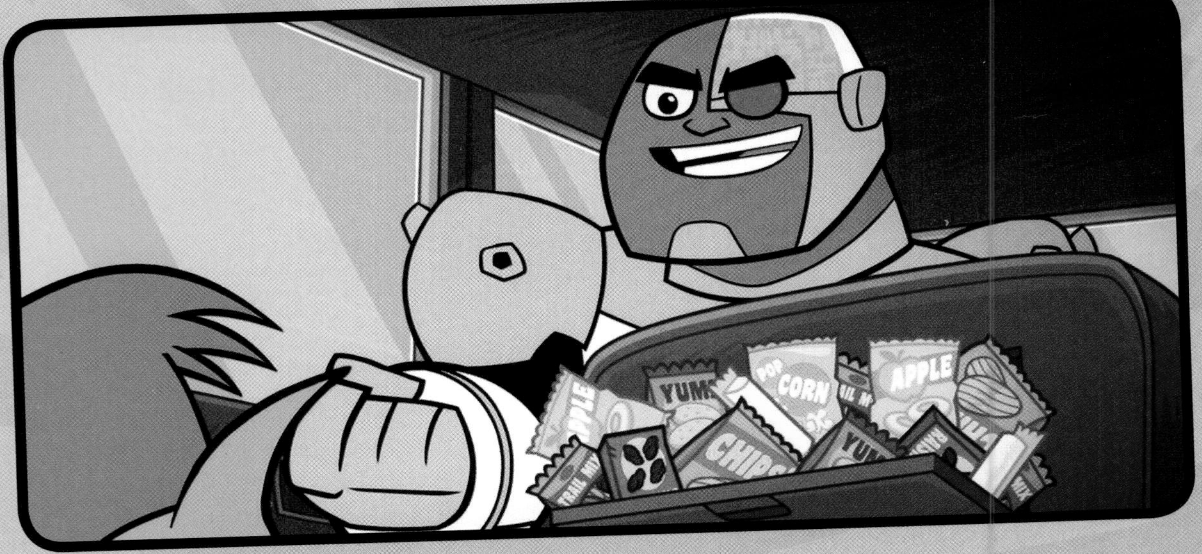
POP
CORN
APPLE
TRAIL MIX

"SNACKS!" Beast Boy scarfs them all and goes ape. He transforms into a giant gorilla, and then he jumps to the roof, ready for action.

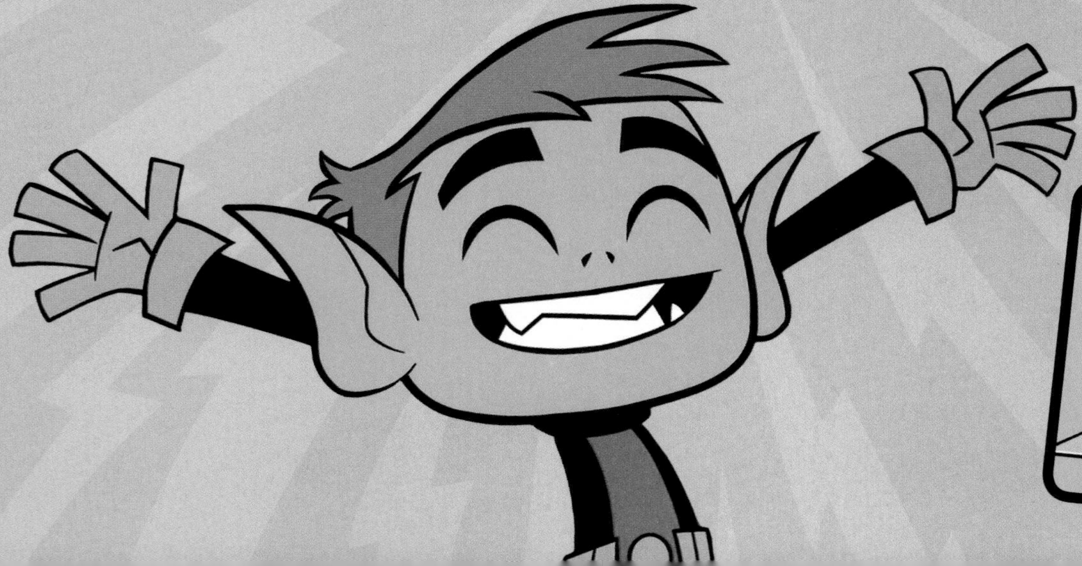

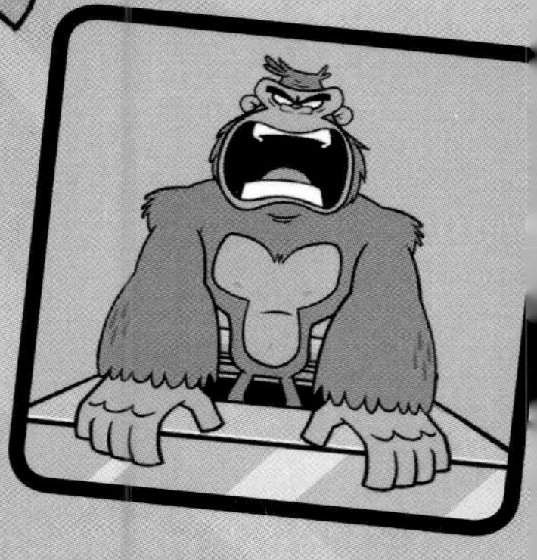

Beast Boy attacks. He punches with all his gorilla might.

But H.I.V.E. keeps coming.

"Nothing's working," says Robin. "What can I do?" asks Raven.

Suddenly, Cyborg has an idea. He grins and says, "Just keep reading."

He jerks the steering wheel back and forth as Raven reads frantically.

But then, car sickness strikes again—Raven can't hold it back. "Out the window! *Out the window!*" cries Cyborg.

"BLEAGH!"

BOOOOM!

Cyborg's plan works! It's a little uncomfortable and gross, but the Titans and their beloved T-Car are safe!

The Titans cheer the best road trip ever. Just then, Cyborg looks at the GPS. "Wait. This is Point B. We made it!"

Robin is confused. "It's just... more road."

"I told you," Cyborg says, patiently explaining himself again. "It's about the *journey*."

Beast Boy, at least, is relieved. "The important thing is, it's over."

"Half over!" Cyborg yells. "Now we gotta go back to Point A. ROAD TRI—"

"Yeah. We're never doing that again," says Robin.

"We live here now," adds Starfire.